Are there rainbow-coloured mountains?

Written by Tom Ottway

Illustrated by Barry Ablett

Collins

What's in this book?

Listen and say

rainbow

mountain

rock

lizard

Download the audio at www.collins.co.uk/839676

up

cable car

ski

snow

wolf

black bear

5

This is Tam and she lives on this mountain. It is called *Mu Cang Chai*. This mountain isn't rainbow coloured!

Tam walks one hour every day in the mountains to school. You can see rice is growing in the fields on the mountain. The highest place is *Fansipan Mountain*.

From the top you can see lots of things.
Tam walked up with her family.
It was fantastic!

Some people come here on holiday.
They go to the top of the mountain in a
cable car.

This is Florine. She lives in a town in the Alp Mountains.

In winter, it snows and the mountains are white! People come here on holiday to ski.

Florine and her brother ski from their house to school. It's five minutes to ski to school.

In summer, there are lots of flowers, and birds in the trees. Florine walks with her brother to school. In the summer they can't ski!

There are lots of rainbow-coloured flowers – yellow, blue, red, pink, white and orange.

This is Zak. He lives in the *Yellowstone National Park*.

There aren't any rainbow-coloured mountains, here!

We have big mountains.

Sometimes the mountains are white with snow.

There are many fantastic animals in these mountains, black bears, brown bears, big cats, wolves and birds.

The mountain forests have a lot of trees. Bears like the trees. Bears are the park's most famous animal. You can often see them in the park!

This beautiful bear is called Zak.

That's my name, too!

This is Carlos. This rainbow mountain is next to his school.

Lots of people come to visit the mountain. You can walk on it. It is made from different rocks.

Rainbow Mountain isn't made from
rainbows but it is the colour of rainbows.

There are also green mountains and white mountains. I would like to go in a cable car or to ski, but I would LOVE to walk on a rainbow.

Picture dictionary

Listen and repeat

cable car   bear   lizard

mountain   rainbow   rock

ski   snow   top   wolf

1 Look and match

2 Listen and say

Collins

Published by Collins
An imprint of HarperCollins*Publishers*
Westerhill Road
Bishopbriggs
Glasgow
G64 2QT

HarperCollins*Publishers*
1st Floor, Watermarque Building
Ringsend Road
Dublin 4
Ireland

William Collins' dream of knowledge for all began with the publication of his first book in 1819.

A self-educated mill worker, he not only enriched millions of lives, but also founded a flourishing publishing house. Today, staying true to this spirit, Collins books are packed with inspiration, innovation and practical expertise. They place you at the centre of a world of possibility and give you exactly what you need to explore it.

10 9 8 7 6 5 4 3 2

ISBN 978-0-00-839676-3

Collins® and COBUILD® are registered trademarks of HarperCollins*Publishers* Limited

www.collins.co.uk/elt

British Library Cataloguing in Publication Data

A catalogue record for this publication is available from the British Library.

Author: Tom Ottway
Illustrator: Barry Ablett (Beehive)
Series editor: Rebecca Adlard
Commissioning editor: Fiona Undrill
Publishing manager: Lisa Todd
Product managers: Jennifer Hall and Caroline Green
In-house editor: Alma Puts Keren
Project manager: Emily Hooton
Editor: Frances Amrani
Proofreaders: Natalie Murray and Michael Lamb
Cover designer: Kevin Robbins
Typesetter: 2Hoots Publishing Services Ltd
Audio produced by id audio, London
Reading guide author: Emma Wilkinson
Production controller: Rachel Weaver
Printed and bound by: GPS Group, Slovenia

Download the audio for this book and a reading guide for parents and teachers at www.collins.co.uk/839676

Collins **peapod readers**

Reader level 4
CEFR Lower A1

What do you know about mountains?

Inspire a love of reading with stories that are written from a child's perspective and will encourage children to discover the world around them. With audio and activities, Peapod Readers are the perfect start to a child's journey into learning English.

- *Before and after reading activities*
- *Picture dictionary*
- *Exam practice for Cambridge Pre A1 Starters, working towards A1 Movers*
- *Reading guide online*

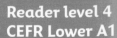 **Download the audio at www.collins.co.uk/839676**

Level	CEFR	Words in story	Headword count
1	Pre A1	50–70	80
2	Pre A1	100–140	200
3	Pre A1	150–230	400
4	Lower A1	250–500	670
5	A1	650–950	820

Non-fiction

ISBN 978-0-00-839676-3

9 780008 396763 >

collins.co.uk/elt

⊆ POWERED BY COBUILD